# Camp Rules!

To Mandy and Ian, who live for camp!—NK

For David and Jason, who built the prettiest
cabin in the world!—J&W

GROSSET & DUNLAP
Published by the Penguin Group
Penguin Group (USA) Inc., 375 Hudson Street, New York,
New York 10014, U.S.A.
Penguin Group (Canada), 90 Eglinton Avenue East, Suite 700, Toronto,
Ontario, Canada M4P 2Y3
(a division of Pearson Penguin Canada Inc.)
Penguin Books Ltd, 80 Strand, London WC2R 0RL, England
Penguin Ireland, 25 St Stephen's Green, Dublin 2, Ireland
(a division of Penguin Books Ltd)
Penguin Group (Australia), 250 Camberwell Road, Camberwell,
Victoria 3124, Australia
(a division of Pearson Australia Group Pty Ltd)
Penguin Books India Pvt Ltd, 11 Community Centre, Panchsheel Park,
New Delhi - 110 017, India
Penguin Group (NZ), 67 Apollo Drive, Mairangi Bay,
Auckland 1311, New Zealand
(a division of Pearson New Zealand Ltd)
Penguin Books (South Africa) (Pty) Ltd, 24 Sturdee Avenue, Rosebank,
Johannesburg 2196, South Africa

Penguin Books Ltd, Registered Offices:
80 Strand, London WC2R 0RL, England

Text copyright © 2007 by Nancy Krulik. Illustrations copyright © 2007 by
John and Wendy. All rights reserved. Published by Grosset & Dunlap, a
division of Penguin Young Readers Group, 345 Hudson Street, New York,
New York 10014. GROSSET & DUNLAP is a trademark of Penguin Group
(USA) Inc. Printed in the U.S.A.

Library of Congress Control Number: 2006033101

ISBN 978-0-448-44542-7          10 9 8 7 6 5 4

# Camp Rules!

by Nancy Krulik • illustrated by John & Wendy

Grosset & Dunlap

# Chapter 1

Dear Pepper,
I am riding on the big yellow bus you saw me get on this morning. It is taking me to Camp Cedar Hill! I miss you already. Right now we are driving in the mountains. There are plenty of trees here. And I've seen a lot of squirrels, bunnies, and chipmunks, too. You would love it!
    I miss you,
    Katie

To: Pepper Carew
Cherrydale, USA

Katie Carew looked down at the note she had just written. Some people might think it was strange that she was sending a postcard to her dog. But Katie didn't care. She wanted to make sure her cocker spaniel knew she was thinking about him while she was away at camp.

An older girl with long brown hair and lots of freckles turned around in her seat and looked at Katie. "Is this your first time at sleepaway camp?" she asked her.

Katie shook her head. "In third grade I went to science camp for three days with my class."

The older girl nodded. "I did that in third grade, too," she said. "But this is different."

Katie already knew that. Katie was going to be at Camp Cedar Hill for two whole weeks. That was fourteen days. Three hundred thirty-six hours. Twenty thousand, one hundred sixty minutes. (Katie had figured that out on her calculator.) When you counted up all those minutes, it sure sounded like forever.

Suddenly, a nervous feeling came over her. It was the same butterflies-in-her-belly feeling she had gotten when she had boarded the camp bus early that morning.

"Do you have any friends who are going to Cedar Hill?" the older girl asked Katie.

Katie shook her head. It was why she was sitting alone on the bus. "I don't know anyone," Katie told her. She bit her lip. Somehow, saying it out loud made it even scarier.

The older girl smiled. "My name is Lexi," she said, holding out her hand. "Now you know someone."

Katie grinned. It made her feel a little better to know someone. Not that they would be in the same bunk or anything. After all, Lexi was a lot older than Katie. But at least there would be a familiar face in the mess hall at lunch.

"I've been going to this camp since I was

eight," Lexi told Katie. "You're going to love it."

"I hope so," Katie told her.

"Do you like sports?" Lexi asked her.

Katie nodded. "But I'm not really great at them," she admitted. "What I really love to do is paint and draw."

"Wait until you see the arts-and-crafts shack," Lexi told her. "It's so cool. They have a pottery wheel, easels, and lots and lots of lanyard." She showed Katie the whistle she had on a long pink and black lanyard. "I made this

last summer."

"It's pretty," Katie said to her.

"We should be there soon," Lexi told Katie. "I just saw the sign for Charlie's Candy Store. That's about a mile from camp. Last year we stopped there during our hike and bought penny candy."

"Yum!" Katie exclaimed.

*Bump. Thump. Bump.* The bus moved up and down as it turned onto an old dirt-and-gravel road.

"We're here, because we're here, because we're here, because we're here!" Lexi started singing with a bunch of other kids.

Katie knew that song. Her best friend Jeremy Fox had taught it to her when their class had gone to science camp.

Jeremy. Suddenly Katie missed him a whole lot. She wished he were going to this camp with her, too.

But of course, that was impossible. Jeremy was a boy. Camp Cedar Hill was just for girls.

The bus climbed up a steep hill and stopped by a big field. Katie looked out the window. There were brown wooden cabins all around her. In the distance she could see tennis courts and a lake.

"This is it," Lexi told her excitedly. "Camp Cedar Hill."

Kids on the bus started cheering. Katie lifted up her backpack and followed Lexi off the bus. A group of counselors were there to greet the girls as they arrived.

"What's your name?" a tall, dark-haired counselor asked Katie.

"Katie Carew," Katie replied nervously.

"Oh goodie, she's mine!" Suddenly a small, thin counselor with a long blond ponytail came bounding over toward Katie. "Hi there, Bumblebee!" she greeted her.

Katie looked at her strangely. "Bumblebee?"

"That's the name of our cabin," the blond counselor said. "We're the Bumblebees. Be careful . . . we sting!" She grabbed Katie and gave her a big bear hug. "I'm Shannon, your counselor."

Katie's eyes opened wide with surprise. Her counselor sure had a lot of energy!

"Come on, the rest of the Bumblebees are already buzzing around the hive," Shannon told Katie. "You'll like them. They're really nice girls."

Katie nodded. She sure hoped so. It would be awful to be trapped in a cabin for twenty thousand, one hundred sixty minutes with girls who weren't nice.

"Your trunk arrived yesterday," Shannon continued. "So you can settle in."

Katie nodded, but she didn't say anything. Shannon was talking enough for both of them, anyway.

# Chapter 2

"We've got a new Bumblebee here!"
Shannon announced, flinging open the
wooden door and walking into the cabin.

Katie looked around nervously. The cabin
was small, with three sets of bunk beds
pushed up against the walls. Beside each pair
of bunk beds was a double cubby.

"Everybody, this is Katie," Shannon said,
introducing her. "Katie, this is everybody."

Katie frowned. That wasn't very helpful.

"Hi, I'm Rainbow," a small girl with a long
light brown ponytail said, coming over to
greet Katie.

"Your name is *Rainbow*?" Katie blurted

out, surprised. Then she blushed. She hadn't meant to hurt the girl's feelings.

But Rainbow didn't seem the least bit upset. "My parents say a rainbow is the most beautiful thing in the whole world," she explained calmly. "That's why they gave me the name."

A tall girl with short dark hair snorted. Then Katie saw her make a face. Katie stared at her in amazement.

"Oh, just ignore her," a girl with curly brown ringlets and silver braces on her teeth said to Rainbow and Katie. "Alicia's always in a bad mood."

Katie nodded. *Okay, so the mean girl's name must be Alicia.*

"I'm Gianna," the girl with the braces introduced herself.

"Did you and Alicia go to camp together before?" Katie asked, wondering how Gianna knew all about her.

Gianna nodded. "We were both here last

summer. This is my third year at Camp Cedar Hill. It's only Alicia's second."

"And last," Alicia groaned. "I told my mother if I got stuck in the baby Bumblebee bunk, I wasn't coming back here ever again. And here I am."

"*We're* babies?" Gianna argued. "*You're* younger than I am."

"Whatever," Alicia said as she continued to unpack her trunk.

"You can have the top bunk," a girl with long beaded earrings and straight strawberry blond hair called to Katie from across the bunk.

"Okay," Katie replied. She stepped over the open trunks and duffel bags until she reached the bed.

"I'm Chelsea," the girl with the earrings told her. "I took that side of the cubby. I hope you don't mind."

Katie looked over toward the double cubby beside her new bed. Chelsea had already

unpacked most of her clothes, her shampoo, soap, and . . . wow!

"You have your own blow-dryer?" Katie asked her in amazement.

"Of course," Chelsea told her. "I never go anywhere without it. My hair gets all crazy and wild if I don't blow-dry it."

Katie smiled at Chelsea. "Your hair does look nice," she told her.

"Thanks," Chelsea replied. "You can use my dryer sometimes if you like."

"Wow!" Katie exclaimed. "Thanks."

Katie pulled her sheets and blankets from her duffel bag and began making her bed. She looked across the way at Rainbow, who also had a top bunk. She was busy tying something to the rafters above her bed.

"What's that?" Katie asked her.

"It's a quartz crystal," Rainbow said, moving to the side so Katie could get a better look at the small clear rock she was hanging above her head. "If you hang it above you, it's supposed to give you positive energy."

"Oh please," Alicia groaned.

"Ignore her," Gianna reminded Rainbow.

"Don't worry. I'm fine," Rainbow said. "Nothing is going to ruin my summer. I can't wait to get out there and be around all this nature. I sure hope we get to camp out one night and sleep under the stars."

"With all these bugs?" Chelsea gasped. "Not me. I'll sleep in here—behind all the screened-in windows."

Katie giggled. "You remind me of my third-grade teacher, Mrs. Derkman," she told Chelsea. "She's really afraid of bugs. You should have seen her when we went on our science-camp trip. She had a million cans of bug spray with her."

"Did it help?" Gianna asked.

Katie nodded. "The bugs stayed away. But she got poison ivy instead!"

Gianna, Chelsea, and Rainbow all laughed, hearing that.

"I hate to break up the gabfest, girls," Shannon said with a smile. "But it's time to head over to the mess hall for some lunch."

"I hope it's something good," Rainbow said.

"You wish!" Alicia groaned.

Katie gulped. "No, she doesn't. She doesn't wish anything!" she shouted out.

The girls in the bunk all stared at her.

"What's wrong with wishes?" Rainbow asked her, looking puzzled.

Katie frowned. What was wrong with wishes?

*A lot.*

# Chapter 3

It all started one horrible day back in third grade. Katie had lost the football game for her team. Then she'd splashed mud all over her favorite jeans. But the worst part of the day came when Katie let out a loud burp—right in front of the whole class. It had been so embarrassing!

That night, Katie wished to be anyone but herself. There must have been a shooting star overhead when she made the wish, because the very next day the magic wind came.

The magic wind was like a really powerful tornado that blew only around Katie. It was so strong, it could blow her right out of her body

*. . . and into someone else's!*

The first time the magic wind appeared, it turned Katie into Speedy, the hamster in her third-grade class. Katie spent the whole morning going round and round on a hamster wheel and chewing on Speedy's wooden chew sticks. They tasted terrible, but Katie couldn't help herself. That's what hamsters did.

The magic wind didn't just turn Katie into animals, though. One time it came and turned her into T-Jon, the rapper in the Bayside Boys. Katie wasn't very good at writing rap music. She'd almost broken up her favorite music group!

And that wasn't the only time the magic wind had caused a musical mess. At the beginning of fourth grade, the magic wind had turned Katie into Mr. Starkey, the school music teacher. The school band had never sounded as bad as when Katie was conducting! It was so awful that all the new kids in the band wanted to quit.

And then there was the time the magic wind came to the Cherrydale Mall and—one, two, switcheroo—changed Katie into Cinnamon, the owner of the candy store. Katie had almost ruined Valentine's Day for everyone by putting the wrong messages on the candy hearts. By the time Cinnamon turned back into herself, everyone was mad at her, *and* at each other. But Cinnamon couldn't remember why.

That was one of the weird things about the magic wind. The people Katie turned into never really remembered too much about what had happened to them.

But Katie never forgot. Which was why she hated wishes so much.

Right now the kids in the bunk were all staring at her, waiting for some explanation of why she had shouted like that. But Katie couldn't tell them the truth. They'd never believe her. Katie wouldn't have believed it, either, if it hadn't kept happening to her.

"I just meant that we're all so hungry, we'll eat anything they put in front of us," Katie explained to her new bunkmates.

There. That sounded sort of believable.

"It'll be pizza bagels," Gianna told her. "It's always pizza bagels on the first day."

"What are pizza bagels?" Chelsea asked.

"They put some cheese and tomato on top of a half a bagel and then cook it in the oven," Gianna explained. "They're kind of soggy, but not too awful."

"Oh good," Rainbow said. "I'm glad it's just cheese and sauce. I don't eat meat."

"Me neither," Katie told her excitedly. "I'm

a vegetarian. I don't eat anything that ever had a face."

Rainbow grinned. "I think we're going to be good pals," she told Katie.

Katie smiled back. She'd been at camp for only a few minutes, and she'd already made a friend. This was going to be an amazing two weeks. She was sure of it.

# Chapter 4

"Oh goodie!" Gianna exclaimed as she sat down at the square wooden table marked "Bumblebees" in the mess hall. "Grape bug juice."

"Bug juice!" Chelsea blurted out, jumping up from the bench. "I'm not drinking anything made with bugs."

Alicia laughed so hard, she snorted. "Oh, come on," she said. "Everyone drinks bugs at camp."

"Stop teasing her," Katie told Alicia.

"There are no bugs in the juice," Gianna assured Chelsea. "It's just called that. It's really just a sugary fruit punch."

"Oh, good," Chelsea said, pouring some of the purple drink into the plastic cup on her tray.

"Hey, girls, you're awfully quiet," Shannon said as she sat down on the bench beside Rainbow. "Where's your Bumblebee spirit?"

"I left it on the bus," Alicia grumbled. "Along with my candy wrappers."

Shannon ignored her and smiled at the rest of the girls. "I feel a cheer coming on!"

she said suddenly. "We are the Bumblebees, couldn't be prouder . . ."

"And if you can't hear us, we'll shout a little louder!" Gianna added. She obviously knew the cheer from last summer. "We are the Bumblebees . . ."

"Couldn't be prouder!" Katie said, joining in. "And if you can't hear us, we'll shout a little louder!"

Before long, all the girls in the mess hall were cheering. It was so loud, Katie could barely make out the names of the other cabins. She thought she heard names like the Sunflowers, the Stingrays, and the Blue Jays, though.

"WE ARE THE BUMBLEBEES, COULDN'T BE PROUDER!" Katie shouted.

Dear Emma,
Camp is awesome. I just came from lunch. You would have loved it. Well, not the food, because that was pretty bad. But we had a lot of fun cheering in the mess hall. It's not like school where you have to be quiet and stay in your seat while you eat. At camp you can scream and cheer and bang on the table. Camp is a lot cooler than school. In fact, camp is cooler than anywhere else!
Wish you were here.
Love, Katie

To: Emma Weber
Cherrydale, USA

"I've never gone swimming in a lake before," Rainbow said as she slipped into her yellow-and-green flowered swimsuit after rest hour was over. "Do you think there are fish in there?"

"There are," Gianna told her. "Plenty of 'em."

"I've got my goggles," Katie said, holding

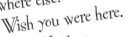

them up. "That way I can open my eyes underwater. Maybe I'll come face-to-face with a fish."

"I can make a fish face," Rainbow told her. She sucked in her cheeks and squished her lips in and out.

"That face will *scare* the fish," Alicia told her.

Rainbow frowned.

"I love your fish face," Katie assured Rainbow. "Will you teach me how to do it?"

"Sure," Rainbow agreed. "Just suck in your cheeks, and then . . ."

Before Katie could make her lips move up and down like a trout, Shannon came bounding into the bunk.

"Okay, girls, it's swim-test time!" the counselor called out cheerfully. "Is everybody ready?"

"Oh, yeah!" Katie exclaimed.

"We want to swim with the fish!" Rainbow seconded.

Shannon looked over at Chelsea. She was still wearing her shorts and T-shirt. "You're not in your bathing suit," she said.

Chelsea shook her head. "I'm not swimming," she declared. "That lake water is terrible for my hair."

"But if you don't take a swim test, you won't be able to go in anywhere but the shallow water," Shannon explained.

"I don't care," Chelsea said. "My hair is worth it."

"Okay, suit yourself," Shannon replied.

"Swimsuit yourself," Rainbow said, giggling as the girls followed Shannon down to the lake.

"We have to swim all the way to that raft?" Katie asked as she stood on the sandy shoreline of the lake a few moments later.

"Only if you want to be a deepwater swimmer," Gianna told her.

"Yeah, you can always swim in the shallow end with the other babies," Alicia said, laughing. "That's what Gianna did all last summer."

"But not this summer," Gianna said proudly. "I've been practicing. I'm going to swim there. In the intermediate area." She pointed to an area of the lake that was sandwiched between two long docks. "The water is deep, but the swim counselors stand on the docks and make sure everyone is okay."

"What do you have to do to get to swim in there?" Rainbow asked her.

Gianna pointed to the raft. "You have to do two laps of crawl, one lap of breaststroke, and one lap of sidestroke," Gianna said.

Katie knew all of those strokes. But she was afraid she might be too tired to do four laps.

"I think I am going to take the intermediate test," she said finally.

"Me too," Rainbow agreed.

"Yeah!" Gianna cheered. "Then we can swim together at free swim."

Alicia rolled her eyes. "I guess I'm the only deepwater swimmer in our bunk," she said, then she dove in and swam out toward the raft. "See you later, Bumblebee babies!"

"Why does she keep saying that?" Rainbow asked. "She's a Bumblebee, just like us."

"Alicia was like that last year, too," Gianna said with a shrug. "She's just mean."

Katie shook her head. "Nobody's just mean," she said quietly. "Not even Alicia."

# Chapter 5

"Boy, pioneering was so much fun!"
Rainbow said at the end of the day as the
girls were getting into their pajamas. "I loved
cooking s'mores over that fire."

Katie nodded in agreement. The graham
crackers, melted chocolate, and marshmallows
had been yummy.

"I've never built a fire before," Chelsea
said. "There's no place to do that in the city."

"Well, you did a really great job!" Katie
said. "The sticks you piled up caught fire right
away."

"I know," Chelsea said proudly. "I can't
wait to write home and tell my parents."

"Big deal, so you piled a bunch of sticks into a pyramid," Alicia groaned. "Like that's really something to write home about."

"It is to me," Chelsea told her. She pulled out a box of stationery. "Anybody want a piece?" she asked. "It smells like bubble gum."

"Oh, cool!" Gianna said. "I'd love to send a letter to my sister on that. Thanks."

"I've got stationery and postcards," Katie said. "Thanks, though."

"My parents would kill me if I sent them a letter on anything but recycled paper," Rainbow explained. "They're really into saving the trees. Thanks anyway, Chelsea."

"How about you?" Chelsea asked, holding her box of stationery out toward Alicia. "You could write your parents to tell them you passed your deepwater test."

"They already knew I would pass," Alicia told her.

"Okay," Chelsea said with a shrug. She started to write her letter.

Katie climbed up in her bed and began to write one, too.

To: Jeremy Fox
Camp Arrowhead
USA

Dear Jeremy,
Hi. How is your camp? Mine's great. I took my swim test today. The bottom of the lake was kind of slimy, but the water was really clean and nice. I didn't see any fish, but there were some little tadpoles swimming around in the shallow part. I guess we're going to have a lot of frogs hopping around here soon.

At night we had a campfire and made s'mores. Do you make those at your camp?

Please write back soon.

Your pal,
Katie

"Okay, Bumblebees, everyone into bed!" Shannon told the girls cheerfully. "It's time for lights-out!"

Katie climbed up into her top bunk and crawled under the covers.

"Good night, sleep tight," Shannon said. "Don't let the bedbugs bite!"

"Oooh. Don't say bugs!" Chelsea groaned.

Shannon laughed. "If you have any problems, there are two counselors on duty outside in the field. Just call for them and they'll come help you."

Katie lay there for a minute, feeling the scratchy camp sheets against her arms and legs. It was weird not being able to sleep in her own bed. Suddenly a big knot began to form in her stomach. She got a lump in her throat.

For the first time all day, Katie felt homesick. She let out a long, sad sigh.

"What's the matter, Katie?" Rainbow asked her.

"I miss my dog," Katie told her. "He always comes into bed with me at night."

"You're so lucky to have a pet," Rainbow said. "My parents think all animals should be free. But I think dogs like living with people."

"I think so, too," Katie said. "Pepper sure likes living with us."

"We can't have pets in our apartment building," Chelsea said sadly.

"I just don't know if I'll be able to fall asleep without him," Katie told the girls.

"Sure you will," Gianna assured her.

"Yeah, we're all really tired," Chelsea said. "You won't be able to stay awake much longer."

"Besides, there are plenty of wild animals around here," Alicia added in a nasty voice. "If you're lucky a big old grizzly bear will crawl into bed with you."

Chelsea gulped. "There are bears here?" she asked nervously.

"I've never seen one," Gianna assured her.

"And this is my third summer. Alicia's just teasing."

"If you say so," Alicia said. "Of course, if it's not a bear, it could be a ghost," she continued. "I did hear about the ghost of an evil camper who roams the campgrounds, looking for unsuspecting campers to haunt."

"Stop it!" Chelsea shouted from her bed. "I hate ghost stories."

"That's all it is," Gianna assured her. "Just a story. There are no ghosts here."

"I hope not," Chelsea said with a shudder.

"I can't stay up another minute," Rainbow told the other girls. "I'll see you all in the morning."

A few minutes later, everything was quiet. Katie lay there in the darkness. She was pretty sure she was the only one in her cabin still awake. And that just made her feel more lonely.

Just then, she heard a scratching noise coming from outside the bunk. It was the kind of noise Pepper made when he wanted to come into her room, but the door was closed.

Katie's eyes opened wide. What if there was a grizzly bear out there?

For a minute, Katie thought about calling out to one of the counselors on duty. Then she changed her mind. There were no grizzly bears at camp. Gianna had told her that.

The scratching was probably just her imagination.

And imagine how badly Alicia would make fun of her if she made a counselor come into their cabin for nothing!

Katie shut her eyes tight and stuck her fingers in her ears to block out the scratching. "There are no bears here," she told herself. "No bears. No bears."

# Chapter 6

The next thing Katie knew, the sun was shining in through the screened windows of the cabin.

"Rise and shine, Bumblebees," Shannon called out loudly. "It's a beautiful day!"

Katie rubbed her eyes and sat up in her bed. It *was* a beautiful day. She could see the sun shining above the rows and rows of pine trees in the woods.

The woods! Suddenly Katie remembered what Alicia had said about the bears that lived there. She thought about the scratching noise she'd heard the night before.

"Uh, Shannon?" Katie asked nervously.

"Yes, Katie?" Shannon answered.

"Are there any bears in the woods here?" Katie continued.

Shannon shook her head. "I've never seen a bear. Not even a bear track. Why?"

"Because I heard something scratching on the side of the cabin last night," Katie told her.

"My guess is you heard a raccoon," Shannon told Katie. "There are lots of them around. That's why you girls shouldn't leave any food out in the bunk. The raccoons will come in and eat it."

"What's wrong with that?" Rainbow asked her. "If the raccoons are hungry, shouldn't we feed them?"

Shannon shook her head. "Raccoons are wild animals. And they can bite," she told Rainbow. "Besides, they really do have plenty to eat out there in the woods—the food nature provides for them, like berries and acorns and bugs."

Chelsea made a face. "Eating bugs. That's nasty."

Shannon giggled. "Not to a raccoon. Now, come on. Our breakfast is ready."

"I sure hope it tastes better than bugs," Chelsea joked.

"Oh my gosh . . . look," Rainbow whispered to Katie after sunset as the girls walked back to the cabin.

Katie looked over to where her friend was pointing. Sure enough, there was a little raccoon chewing on some wild berries that grew in the dark wooded area behind the cabin.

"He's so cute," Rainbow said quietly. "I think he's a baby." She took a step in his direction.

"Don't," Katie warned. "You'll scare him. And remember what Shannon said."

"But he looks so soft and cuddly,"

Rainbow insisted. "Look at his little black mask and those rings around his tail."

"He's a wild animal," Katie reminded her.

"Do you see his mom anywhere?" Rainbow asked.

Katie looked into the woods. She didn't see a mother raccoon anywhere. That made her sad. "Poor little thing. He's all alone out in the woods, with no one to take care of him."

"Maybe *we* could take care of him," Rainbow suggested. "You know, feed him."

"But Shannon said we couldn't bring food inside the bunk," Katie reminded her.

"And we won't," Rainbow assured Katie. "We'll leave his food *outside* the bunk."

A big smile came over Katie's face. "Great idea!" she said. "We're going to the canteen tonight for evening activity. I think I'll get some peanut-butter crackers for him."

"And I'll get him popcorn," Rainbow added. "We can leave the food right here."

Katie watched as the raccoon licked his front paws clean. "You know, if he's going to be our pet, we should give him a name," she said.

"Can I name him?" Rainbow asked her. "I've never had a pet before."

"Sure," Katie agreed. "What should we call him?"

Rainbow thought for a minute. Then, finally, she said, "Rocky. We'll call him Rocky Raccoon. It's the name of an old song my parents like."

"Rocky Raccoon," Katie repeated. "I like it."

"We'd better go wash up or we'll miss canteen," Rainbow said.

"Okay," Katie agreed. She turned and headed toward the cabin door. "Bye, Rocky," she added.

"Let's not tell anyone about our pet," Rainbow told Katie.

"Not a soul," Katie agreed. "He's our secret."

But someone else already knew all about Rocky. She had been hiding behind a tree the whole time. And she'd heard every word Katie and Rainbow had said.

"Hey, do you hear that?" Chelsea asked that night as the girls climbed into bed.

"It's probably just a raccoon," Gianna told her. "It's just hungry and looking for food, just like Shannon said."

*Not so hungry*, Katie thought happily to herself. After all, she and Rainbow had left him plenty of goodies to munch on. "Raccoons usually come out at night," she said instead.

"Someone must be feeding him," Alicia remarked. "Otherwise he would go away."

"There's no food in our bunk," Rainbow told her.

"Definitely nothing *in* here," Katie seconded.

Alicia shrugged. "I'm just saying that if the raccoon couldn't get food near our bunk, it would leave."

"He's not bothering anyone," Rainbow said.

"He's bothering me," Chelsea told her. "That scratching is driving me crazy."

Gianna giggled. "Well, just put a pillow over your ears and drown it out!" she shouted, hitting Chelsea with her pillow.

"I'll get you for that," Chelsea said, leaping out of bed and slamming Gianna with her pillow.

Katie grabbed her pillow and climbed down from her bed. She reached up and hit Rainbow in the face with the pillow.

Rainbow sat up in her bed, grabbed her pillow, and leaped from her top bunk. "Eeyaah!" she yelled, coming up behind Katie and hitting her on the head.

Within seconds, all the girls in the bunk were involved in a big pillow fight. All the girls except Alicia, that is. They'd all been afraid to hit her with their pillows.

But Alicia didn't seem to want to be part of the fun, anyway. "Babies," she mumbled in a grouchy voice as she rolled over on her side.

# Chapter 7

"Keep your eye on the ball, Katie," Gianna said as she served the tennis ball over the net the next afternoon. Katie and Gianna had both signed up to play tennis for their first activity. Gianna was really good. Katie wasn't. But she was trying.

"I played tennis a lot last summer," Gianna said. "That's how I got so good. If you practice, you'll get good at it, too."

*Boing.* The ball hit the center of Katie's racket and bounced over the net. "I did it!" she shouted excitedly.

"Yeah!" Gianna cheered as she hit the ball back to Katie. "Try it again."

*Whoosh*. Katie swung at the ball and then missed it completely.

"Oh, well, you're still getting better," Gianna assured her kindly.

"I'm getting thirsty, too," Katie said.

"I know what you mean," Gianna agreed. "Let's go to the canteen and get some juice."

Katie nodded. That was a good idea. She'd be able to get Rocky a few snacks there, too.

It seemed like all of the Bumblebees were hot and thirsty. By the time Katie and Gianna arrived at the canteen, Alicia, Chelsea, and Rainbow were already there. Katie went over to the small store and bought herself a juice, a candy bar, and some peanut-butter crackers. (The crackers were actually for Rocky.) Then she sat down on a log and began to drink her juice.

Alicia came over a minute later. "Oh, yum," Alicia said, eyeing Katie's canteen goodies.

"Didn't you get anything?" Katie asked, looking at Alicia's empty hands.

Alicia smiled. "I just bought a juice. I don't need to get anything else since you're going to give me your chocolate bar and crackers."

"Why would she do that?" Rainbow asked, coming up behind Katie.

"The same reason you're going to give me that ice-cream sandwich you just bought," Alicia said with a sly grin.

"Huh?" Rainbow asked.

"If you don't give me the food, I'll tell Shannon that you guys are feeding that raccoon behind the bunk," Alicia told her. "She's not going to like that."

"How did you know about Rocky?" Rainbow asked her. She didn't even try to deny it.

"That doesn't matter," Alicia told her. "The point is, I know about your pet raccoon. And if you don't give me those snacks, Shannon's going to find out, too."

Katie frowned. She didn't want Shannon to make her stop feeding Rocky. She handed her snacks to Alicia.

"Smart move," Alicia said as she took Rainbow's ice-cream sandwich as well.

✕ ✕ ✕

"What is her problem, anyway?" Katie asked.

"I don't know, and I don't care. Do you want to go out in a canoe?" Rainbow asked

Katie a little while later as the girls walked toward the lake.

Before Katie could answer, her stomach rumbled. She was kind of hungry, because Alicia had eaten her snack. Still, that was a small price to pay to keep Rocky a secret. After all, the poor little orphaned raccoon really needed them.

Katie nodded. "I think Gianna and Chelsea are going canoeing, too."

"We can race!" Rainbow said.

Katie nodded excitedly. Then she stopped. "If we're all out in canoes, what's Alicia going to do?"

Rainbow shook her head. "I don't know. Probably go kayaking by herself. She doesn't like to be around other people, anyway— unless it's to bully someone."

Katie nodded. That was pretty much all Alicia did.

But not Katie. She was busy with all sorts of activities. Soon it would be her favorite part of the day: choice time. That was when they all split up and went to the activities they wanted to.

"I signed up for arts and crafts," Katie told Rainbow. "Then volleyball and archery. What activities are you going to?"

"I'm going on a nature hike," she said. "It's three hours long, so I won't be back until dinnertime."

"Sounds like fun," Katie said.

Rainbow reached into her pocket. "I was saving this to give to Rocky for his dinner," she said, pulling out a granola bar. "But since I won't be here, can you give it to him?"

"Sure," Katie said. "I'll leave it for him before I go for afternoon swim."

"Perfect!" Rainbow said. Then she started running toward the lake. "Last one to the lake is a rotten egg!" she shouted.

# Chapter 8

*Grrrowl.*

Katie's stomach rumbled as she walked
from the volleyball courts to the archery
targets that evening. Volleyball sure could
make a girl hungry. And there was still an
activity period to go before dinner.

Just then, Katie remembered Rainbow's
granola bar, the one for Rocky. She pulled it
from her pocket and looked at it for a minute.
It was a big bar for such a little raccoon.
Katie was sure he wouldn't mind sharing it
with her.

Quickly Katie ripped the paper off and
took a bite of the granola bar. *Mmm.* That

was good. All chewy and honey-flavored. Maybe just one more bite . . .

A moment later, the entire granola bar was gone. Katie had eaten the whole thing. There was nothing left for Rocky.

"That wasn't a very nice thing for me to do," Katie murmured quietly. She felt pretty bad. She was also pretty thirsty. She should probably stop at her cabin and get a drink of water before going to archery.

Katie was just a few feet from the Bumblebee cabin when she spotted Rocky. He was sleeping high up in a tree, far from the reach of any humans.

Just seeing Rocky made Katie feel guilty about having eaten his snack. He was really going to have to search hard for food tonight. And it was all her fault.

Katie was too ashamed to even look at Rocky. Feeling sad, she began to walk up the stairs to her empty cabin.

Before she could get very far, a cool breeze

began blowing against Katie's neck. She looked around her. The leaves in the trees were completely still. So were the wildflowers that grew all around her bunk. The wind wasn't blowing on them.

In fact, the wind wasn't blowing anywhere, except around Katie! Oh no! This was no ordinary wind. The magic wind had followed Katie all the way to Camp Cedar Hill.

The magic wind grew stronger, circling wildly around Katie like a fierce tornado. It picked up speed, blowing harder and harder. *WHOOSH!* Katie was sure it would blow her away. She shut her eyes tight and tried not to cry.

And then it stopped. Just like that. The magic wind was gone. And so was Katie Carew.

She'd turned into somebody else. One, two, switcheroo!

But who?

Katie opened her eyes slowly. The sunlight seemed very, very bright to her all of a sudden. It was almost blinding. She blinked a few times and then used her front claws to scratch an itch on her ear.

Wait a minute. Katie didn't have claws. She had fingers and toes . . . or at least she used to. Now she had claws! Sharp ones!

Katie looked down. Sure enough, her red sneakers were gone. That made sense since her feet were gone, replaced by paws.

*Raccoon* paws!

Oh no! The magic wind had turned her into Rocky!

Katie gulped. It had been fun having a raccoon for a pet, but she didn't want to be one. Especially not one that was as hungry as Rocky was. Katie's tiny raccoon tummy rumbled with hunger.

Now Katie really wished she'd saved that granola bar. But now there was no granola bar in sight. At least she didn't think so. It was hard for Katie to see anything. Her little raccoon eyes were meant to see in the dark, not the sunlight. The light made her head hurt.

And she was kind of sleepy. She wasn't
supposed to wake up until nighttime. Well,
actually, *Rocky* wasn't supposed to wake up
until then. But since Katie *was* Rocky . . .

Katie couldn't think about that now.
She couldn't think about anything but how
hungry she was. Her little raccoon belly was
completely empty.

Katie picked her head up for a moment
and sniffed at the air. *Mmmm* . . . something
smelled really good. Sweet, like berries.

She turned her head in the direction of
the scent. Sure enough, there was a mulberry
bush a few feet away. Quickly she shinnied
down the tree trunk and scurried over to the
mulberries.

One by one, Katie used her raccoon paws
to pick the berries off the bush and smush
them up. Katie didn't really know why she was
doing that. She had a feeling it had something
to do with checking that there wasn't
anything sharp or dangerous in the food, but

she couldn't be sure. It was just some raccoon thing.

*Mmm* . . . the mulberries tasted delicious. Katie swallowed the mushed berries and licked every bit of the sweet juice from her front paws. She didn't want to leave a drop.

The berries were heavenly, but they weren't very filling. She needed something bigger to eat. Just then she spotted some grubs crawling around a rotting log. She just had to eat them.

Katie stopped for a minute. Grubs. *Yuck.* Why was she so eager to eat disgusting, wormlike bugs?

Because she was a *raccoon*. That's why. And even though eating squiggly, wiggly bugs wasn't something Katie would ordinarily do, they were definitely on Rocky's menu. Quickly Katie scurried over to the log and scooped up a handful of grubs. She used her front paws to squish them up. Then she popped them in her mouth.

Katie sighed. You couldn't be a vegetarian when you were a raccoon.

They ooey-gooey grubs slimed straight down Katie's throat. To her raccoon tongue, they actually tasted pretty yummy. Maybe there were some more inside the log. Katie reached in with one of her front paws and felt around.

No. No more grubs. But the inside of the log did feel kind of soft. And it was dark in there. Katie was feeling tired. She thought about crawling inside the log and taking a nap . . .

Suddenly there was a slight shift in the breeze. Katie lifted up her little raccoon head and sniffed at the air.

*Mmm.* Something sure smelled good. Kind of sweet and creamy. Like cookies. She sniffed at the air again. The smell was coming from the Bumblebee bunk.

There was food in there. *Good food.*

Katie just had to have it!

# Chapter 9

The door to the cabin was shut. But Katie wasn't giving up. Whatever was inside that cabin was too good.

Katie used her teeth to pull at the bottom of the door. It opened just a crack. But that was enough for Katie to slip her little raccoon paw in and pull the door open a little wider. She snuck right inside.

The cabin was empty. Perfect. No one to shoo her away. It was just the snack and her.

But where was the food? Whoever had been sneaking it into the cabin was smart enough not to leave it out for all to see.

Katie padded around the cabin for a

moment, sniffing the air as she moved.

It wasn't in her cubby—she already knew that. And one good sniff of Chelsea's side of the cubby let her know there was no food in there, either—although that strawberry lip gloss sure smelled sweet.

But Katie didn't want shiny lips. She was looking for food. And as she passed by Alicia's cubby, she knew she'd found it.

The sweet smell of peanuts and sugar was coming through plain and clear. There was definitely some sort of candy in that cubby. It was in the bottom shelf. Perfect! Katie wouldn't even have to climb to get it!

She reached her paw into the cubby and began to yank Alicia's clothes out of the way. Her raccoon claws finally landed on something hard. There, hidden inside Alicia's green-and-white Camp Cedar Hill T-shirt was a half-eaten pack of cookies.

Oh yeah! *Supper time!*

Quickly Katie climbed inside the shirt and

took a cookie in her front paws. She opened her raccoon jaws wide. But before she could even take one bite, the cabin door swung open.

"AHHH!" From inside her T-shirt dining room, Katie could hear Chelsea's screams.

"That T-shirt!" Chelsea yelled. "It's moving all by itself. It's a *ghost*! The evil camper ghost! Alicia wasn't making it up!"

Katie remembered how scared of ghosts Chelsea was. She wanted to show her that she wasn't a ghost at all. She was just a little, hungry raccoon.

Katie struggled to climb out of the shirt. But the more she rolled and wriggled to get free, the more she got tangled in Alicia's big camp T-shirt.

"The ghost is going crazy!" Chelsea cried out.

"Chels, calm down," Katie heard her counselor's voice. "There's no such thing as ghosts."

Suddenly Katie heard a loud whirring noise. Chelsea screamed again. Her hair dryer was in her left hand. A blast of hot air shot right at Katie.

"What are you doing?" Shannon shouted.

"I'm trying to blow it out of here!" Chelsea shouted.

"You're blow-drying a ghost?" Shannon asked, amazed.

"I thought you said there were no such things as ghosts?" Chelsea demanded.

"There aren't," Shannon said. "I just meant that . . ."

At just that minute, Katie managed to poke her little raccoon head out of the neck of the shirt.

"AHHH!" Now it was Shannon's turn to scream. "It's a raccoon! I hate raccoons!"

Shannon could scream even louder than Chelsea. The loud shouts, the whirring of the hair dryer, and all that hot air were making Katie very scared. Her baby raccoon heart

was beating fast. She dropped the cookie, wriggled out of the shirt, and jumped up on top of one of the beds.

"Get out! Get out!" Shannon screamed, picking up a broom and trying to shoo Katie to the door. Katie leaped out of the way of the swinging broom and scrambled across the floor, knocking over a trash can as she ran.

"Get out! Get out!" Shannon shouted again.

Katie gulped. Her counselor was swinging the broom wildly. She didn't care if she hit Katie or not.

Of course, Shannon didn't know she was Katie. She thought she was a raccoon. Not that that made it any better.

Katie had to get out of there, and fast! She leaped up onto a top bunk and looked for a way to escape.

There was only one way out—through the windows. But they weren't open. And she had no time to figure out how to open the latch with her paws. So Katie escaped the only way she knew how.

*Scratch. Scratch. Scratch.* In an instant Katie had used her sharp raccoon claws to tear a hole in the screen window. A hole just big enough for a raccoon to slip through.

And in a moment Katie was free!

But Shannon was right behind her. "Raccooooon!" she shouted out. "Raccooooon!"

Luckily, Katie spotted the hollow log where she'd been snacking a few minutes before. She leaped into the hole and pulled her head down low.

It was cool and damp inside the log. And if Katie wasn't mistaken, there was something crawling up and down her leg. It was gross in there. But at least she was safe.

At least for now.

A few moments later Katie heard voices outside her log.

"I'm not sure where that raccoon went,

but it better not show up again," Katie heard Shannon say.

"Yeah, it better not," Chelsea echoed. "I'm just glad it wasn't a ghost. But it sure disappeared like one."

"It's probably hiding in a tree or a hollow log," someone answered Shannon. Katie thought she sounded like Carrie, the nature counselor. "The thing is, raccoons won't usually go near people unless they're sick or frightened," Carrie explained to Shannon and Chelsea. "That's why I always tell kids to stay away from them. If a kid gets bitten by a raccoon, it means a trip to the hospital."

"This raccoon did seem a little crazy," Shannon said. "It wasn't acting like a normal raccoon."

Katie frowned. That was for sure. Maybe because this raccoon was actually a ten-year-old girl!

"Don't worry, I'll catch it," Carrie assured her. "I'll put a little peanut butter in this trap, and sooner or later the raccoon will come out to get it."

"You won't hurt the raccoon, will you?" Chelsea asked her.

"Oh, no," Carrie told her. "I wouldn't hurt any animal. This is a humane trap. The raccoon just gets stuck in this little cage. Then I'll take it far out in the woods."

After a few more minutes, Katie heard footsteps moving away from the hollow log. When she was certain everyone was gone, she poked her little head out of the log.

Sure enough, the smell of peanut butter was wafting through the air. But this time Katie was too smart to go after it. She knew where the peanut butter was hidden. It was in that little cage.

She couldn't get caught in that. After all, Katie wasn't really a raccoon. She was a fourth-grade girl in a raccoon's body. Suppose she was stuck in that cage when the magic wind came back to turn her into Katie again?

The real Katie would never fit in that tiny cage.

And the real Rocky wouldn't like it very much in there, either.

# Chapter 10

Katie hopped out of the log and scampered up to a branch on a nearby tree—well out of the reach of any traps or counselors. She needed time to think.

Katie knew she had to get away from there before Shannon and the kids came back. But if she ran off into the woods, she was liable to get lost.

What if she got lost in the woods forever, walking around and around in circles and never finding her way back to camp? She could be stuck here forever. She'd never see Cherrydale again.

Suddenly Katie was very homesick.

If Katie were a human she might have

started to cry. But raccoons didn't cry. They could, however, feel scared and alone. And that was exactly how Katie felt.

Just then Katie felt a cool breeze blowing on her back. Her whiskers twitched slightly. There was a change in the air.

It was actually getting kind of chilly. Now *that* was weird for summer. Katie leaped out of the tree and started back toward the hollow log. At least she would be warmer there.

But a log was no match for this wind. This was the magic wind. And before Katie could crawl into the hole in the log, it began blowing wildly—only around Katie! The tornado circled fiercely now. She shut her little raccoon eyes and dug her claws into the log, holding on tight—trying not to get blown out into the deep, dark woods.

And then it stopped. Just like that.

Katie Carew was back. And so was Rocky. He was standing a few feet from her, with his head up in the air.

Katie watched as he sniffed at the air for a moment and then began running toward the smell of the peanut butter.

"Rocky, no!" she shouted out. "It's a trap!"

The sound of Katie's voice startled Rocky. He jumped slightly and scampered up a tree—away from the trap.

Rocky was safe now. But Katie knew that wouldn't last long. Sooner or later the smell of that yummy peanut butter would be too much for him. He would come down and try to get it. And then he would be trapped.

Katie couldn't bear the thought of Rocky being stuck in a cage—even if it was just for a little while. Wild animals didn't belong in cages—*ever*.

She glanced over at Rocky. He looked so confused, as if he had no idea what had been happening to him.

Which of course he didn't. The people (and animals) Katie turned into never did.

But if Rocky was confused now, imagine

how he would feel if Carrie took him someplace where he'd never been before. He would be lost and alone.

Maybe forever.

That wasn't fair at all! Katie was going to have to find a way to get Rocky to a safe place where he would be happy.

But how?

This mess was too big for Katie to fix on her own. She knew that. She would need assistance.

There was only one person who could help her: someone who wasn't afraid of animals. Someone who liked animals almost as much as she did.

Quickly Katie ran off toward the nature shack. There wasn't a moment to spare.

"I know we were wrong," Katie apologized to Carrie after she explained about leaving food for Rocky.

"Yes, you were," Carrie told her.

"But he was so tiny and all alone," Katie said. "Like he was lost or something. We just wanted to take care of him."

"Well, we'll get Rocky," Carrie said. "And I'll take him where he'll be safe and away from us."

"You can't put him in a cage," Katie pleaded. "That would be like punishing him. He didn't do anything wrong. Rainbow and I did."

"We have to get him out of here, Katie," Carrie insisted. "We have to make sure the campers stay safe."

"There has to be another way," Katie tried again.

Carrie thought for a minute. "Maybe there is," she said. "Come with me."

That evening Katie found herself hiking through the dark woods with Carrie by

her side. With
every few steps they took,
Carrie dropped a few bits of
animal feed. Much to Katie's amazement, soon
Rocky appeared and followed behind them. He
stayed far away—he was very scared of people.
But he was following them just the same,
eating the feed as he went.

Before long there were so many big, thick
trees Katie could barely see the sky. The
woods were scary at night. Katie was glad she
was with a grown-up. It would be terrible to be
alone out here. Katie sighed. Rocky probably
felt pretty lonely right now.

It was as if Carrie realized what Katie was
thinking, because she said, "If we can get him
far enough out into the woods, maybe he can
find some other raccoons."

"What if we can't?" Katie asked her.

Carrie stopped short and pointed her flashlight down to the ground. The light fell on some animal tracks. The front-paw tracks were short, with five fingerlike lines. The back-paw tracks were longer and thinner. But they had fingerlike lines, too.

"Raccoon tracks!" Katie cried out.

"*Shhh . . .*" Carrie whispered. She pointed to a nearby tree. "I think this story is going to have a happy ending."

Katie looked toward where Carrie was pointing. A big mother raccoon and her baby were sitting on a low branch. The baby looked a lot like Rocky.

"Is that Rocky's mom?" Katie asked her.

Carrie shrugged. "Could be. Anyway, he won't be alone with her here. She'll take care of him. He's got a family now."

Katie nodded.

"Come on, we'd better get back to camp," Carrie told her.

"Okay," Katie said. She felt kind of sad. She was going to miss Rocky. And so would Rainbow.

But thanks to Katie, Rocky was going to be a very happy raccoon. As she and Carrie headed back through the dark woods toward Camp Cedar Hill, Katie began to cheer. "I'm Katie Kazoo. Couldn't be prouder. And if you can't hear me, I'll shout a little louder!"

# Chapter 11

Alicia's angry voice was the first thing Katie heard when she entered the Bumblebee cabin.

"Who knocked all my stuff onto the floor?" Alicia demanded angrily.

"Not me," said Chelsea, who stood by the bathroom mirror brushing her long, silky hair. "I was playing basketball."

"It wasn't me," Gianna told Alicia. "I was at arts and crafts, cooking, and tennis this afternoon. I haven't been back to the bunk since lunch."

"And Rainbow's on that hike," Alicia recalled. She stomped across the cabin toward where Katie was standing. "Which means it had to be you!" she shouted. "You're the one who dumped all my clothes out of my cubby."

Katie bit her lip. That was sort of true. Except she hadn't been Katie when she'd done it.

"Alicia, stop yelling at everyone," Shannon said as she walked into the cabin. "It's your own fault that your clothes are on the floor. You left food in your cubby. A raccoon came in here looking for it. Then he escaped through that window." She pointed to the torn screen.

"A raccoon!" Alicia gulped. She knew she was in trouble.

"And that's why tonight, while the rest of us are at a campfire roasting marshmallows, you're going to be here, helping someone from maintenance fix the window," Shannon continued.

Alicia said nothing and kicked at the ground. Katie could tell she was upset about missing the campfire.

Katie bit her lip. After all, the torn window was as much her fault as it was Alicia's. She should probably be staying behind to help with the work, too.

But Katie could never explain how she'd torn the window to Shannon and the other Bumblebees. They'd never believe her.

Still, Katie felt pretty bad about what had happened. "Let me help you fold your clothes," Katie offered.

"Why? So you can snoop through my stuff?" Alicia demanded.

"No," Katie said. "I just thought you could use the help. I could fix the window with you, too, if you want."

"I don't need anything from you, Bumblebee baby," Alicia snapped back.

Alicia was going to take the punishment all by herself. And even though Alicia was a big mean bully, Katie still felt kind of guilty about it.

"Okay, everybody, mail call!" Shannon shouted a few minutes later as she returned to the bunk with a pile of letters and packages. The girls all raced over to see if they'd gotten anything.

"Here's a big box for you, Chelsea," Shannon said, handing her a package. "There's a package for Rainbow, too. You got a postcard, Gianna. And there are *three* letters for you, Katie."

Katie smiled and took the three envelopes from Shannon's hand. She could tell who they were from right away.

One letter was from her mom. She always wrote SWAK (which meant Sealed With A Kiss) on the back.

The one with glitter stickers all over it had to be from Suzanne. No one loved glitter more than Suzanne Lock.

The third letter was from George Brennan. Katie could tell because he'd written jokes all over the envelope. On the front he'd written Katie Kazoo before crossing out Kazoo and spelling Carew over it.

"Hey, you guys, where do baby dogs sleep when they camp out?" Katie read aloud.

"Where?" Gianna asked.

"In a pup tent!" Katie answered, laughing.

Shannon chuckled. "That's a good one, Katie."

"Ooh, look at what my cousin sent me," Chelsea squealed suddenly. She reached into her box and pulled out a pile of hair ribbons. "They're from my favorite store in the city."

"Wow, can I wear one to the campfire tonight?" Gianna asked, running over to Chelsea's bed.

"Sure," Chelsea told her. "How about this red ribbon?"

"Thanks!" Gianna exclaimed.

"This headband matches your eyes, Katie," Chelsea said, holding up a green-and-white striped stretchy band. "You should wear it tonight."

Katie smiled. "Gee, thanks," she said.

Alicia, who didn't have any mail, rolled her eyes. "Why are you guys getting all dressed up for a campfire?" she groaned. "This isn't the city, Chelsea. You don't have to look all fancy. Besides, those ribbons and headbands are going to smell like smoke if you wear them."

"That's okay," Chelsea said, reaching in

and pulling out a bag of clips. "There are plenty more where they came from."

"Friends, friends, friends we will always be. Whether in fair or in dark stormy weather, Camp Cedar Hill will keep us together . . ."

Katie smiled as she and Rainbow wrapped their arms around each other and sang. She looked over at Gianna and Chelsea. They really were all friends. Just like the song said. And it was pretty amazing, because they'd only been at camp for three days, but already Katie felt as if she had known them her whole life.

"Ahhh! My marshmallow's on fire!" Chelsea yelled out suddenly. She held up a metal skewer with a burning marshmallow on top.

"Blow it out!" Rainbow shouted.

Chelsea blew hard. The fire went out. All that was left was a blackened marshmallow.

"Oh man, it's ruined," she said.

"They taste best that way," Gianna assured her. "Try it."

Chelsea looked doubtful. But she pulled the ooey-gooey burned marshmallow from the skewer and took a bite anyway. "Mmmm," she purred. "This is good."

"Told ya," Gianna replied. "The counselor I had my first year here taught me that."

"We're so lucky to have you in our bunk," Chelsea said. "You know all about this place."

"We're all lucky to be in the same bunk," Gianna told her.

Just then an older girl walked over to where the Bumblebees were sitting. "Hi, Katie," she said.

"Hi, Lexi," Katie greeted her.

"See, I told you you would have a great time here," Lexi said.

"You were right," Katie agreed. "Are you having fun?"

"The best summer ever," Lexi told her. "I

learned how to water-ski today. You'll get to do that, too, when you're in the Stingray cabin."

"I can't wait!" Katie exclaimed. And she meant it. She knew she wanted to come back to Camp Cedar Hill every summer for as long as she was a kid. This place was the best.

As Lexi walked away, Katie put another marshmallow on her skewer. "Come on, you guys," she said to her fellow Bumblebees. "Let's see who can toast the gooeyest one!"

# Chapter 12

*Drip. Drip. Drip.*

The rain was the first thing Katie heard when she woke up in the morning. She lifted up her head and looked out the window. Sure enough, the leaves on the trees were heavy and wet. The ground was covered with soggy puddles.

Camp didn't look nearly as pretty in the rain. It was just a big, wet, muddy mess. Katie pulled the covers over her head and sighed.

The heavy downpour had woken Alicia, too. "Man, this stinks!" she groaned. "I hate rainy days. You can't play ball or go boating or anything. I'll be stuck in this cabin with

Bumblebee babies all day."

Katie rolled her eyes. She didn't get upset when Alicia called them all babies anymore. Nobody did. They ignored her.

"Sometimes we go to the movies or the bowling alley in town when it rains," Gianna recalled. "Remember, Alicia?"

"That's only if it rains for a few days in a row," Alicia reminded her.

"My hair is going to frizz," Chelsea moaned, sitting up in her bed. "I always look like a mess when it rains."

Katie frowned. This was the first time she'd woken up unhappy at camp. Only Rainbow had a big smile on her face. "This is awesome!" she exclaimed, leaping out of bed.

"Okay, I think she's finally gone crazy," Alicia grumbled as Rainbow pulled a bathing suit from her cubby.

"I don't think we're going to be swimming today," Katie told Rainbow kindly.

"Oh, I'm not going swimming," Rainbow

told her. "I'm taking a shower."

"In your bathing suit?" Gianna asked.

Rainbow nodded. "I'm going to take a shower in the rain."

"Cool!" Katie exclaimed and leaped out of bed. "Wait for me."

"Me too!" Chelsea cried. "I'll bet rainwater is really good for your hair."

"Wow. I've never done this before," Gianna told Rainbow. "Not once in the three years I've been here."

"Are you coming, Alicia?" Katie asked as she grabbed her shampoo bottle and headed for the door.

Alicia sighed. "Well, I guess I have to shower anyway," she said, slowly getting out of her bed.

By the time Alicia made it outside, the other Bumblebees were all lathered up. Shannon walked out on the porch and smiled at her girls. "Now that's the Bumblebee spirit," she said. "When life gives you lemons,

you make lemonade."

"I'm glad it's not raining lemonade,"
Chelsea told her. "That would make my hair
really sticky."

Katie giggled. Then she waved her hands high in the air, wiggled her hips, and did a little happy dance.

At camp even the rain was awesome!

Dear Suzanne,

You won't believe what I learned how to do today. My friend Chelsea taught me how to French braid my hair! When you wear your hair that way you look so grown-up! I'll show you how to do it when I get home.

I also found out that rainwater makes your hair really shiny. That's right. I actually took a shower in the rain! You can get pretty clean that way—your entire body except your feet, which get kind of muddy. You have to rinse them off after.

Write back soon.

Love,

Katie

# Chapter 13

The next day the sun was shining brightly. Katie and the other Bumblebees were busy all day long.

Katie had had an especially busy day. She'd played a game of softball during athletics, gone out on the lake in a sailboat in boating, made tea out of dandelions in pioneering, and played flashlight tag during evening activities.

Before bed, everybody wrote letters. Everybody except Alicia.

"You guys want to have some *real* fun?" she asked the girls right before lights-out.

"I had real fun all day," Gianna told her. "Now I want to get some real sleep."

"Me too," Katie agreed, putting away her stationery. "I'm bushed."

"You guys are so boring," Alicia said. "Let's go bunk hopping."

"What's that?" Katie asked.

"Sneaking out of the bunk and visiting other cabins," Alicia told her.

"That's not allowed," Katie told her. "We're supposed to stay here after lights-out."

"Come on," Alicia said. "Don't be such a goody-goody."

Katie frowned. Sometimes her friends at school called her that, too.

And she hated it. She just believed in following rules, that was all.

"It's no big deal," Alicia told the girls. "They *expect* us to do it. It's a camp tradition."

Chelsea looked over at Gianna. "Is it?" she asked.

Gianna shrugged. "I've heard a lot of the older girls talking about how they go bunk hopping some nights."

"Exactly," Alicia agreed. "And the Bumblebees can't do anything the older girls can."

"She's got a point," Rainbow said. "We're only a few months younger than the Sea Horses. But they got to go on that sleepover canoe trip and we didn't."

"Yeah, and didn't that friend of Katie's tell us the Stingrays get to water-ski?" Rainbow recalled.

Alicia nodded. "I'm a better swimmer than most of them, but I don't get to do that," she pointed out.

"It's not fair!" Rainbow shouted.

"I know," Alicia said. "Which is why I think we should go bunk hopping."

"Me too," Chelsea agreed.

"I'm in," Rainbow said. "It's a matter of principle."

"Well," Gianna said slowly. "When you put it that way . . . Let's just not get caught."

"We won't," Alicia said as she grabbed her

flashlight. "We're too smart for that."

Katie watched as one by one her friends slipped their sneakers on and took out their flashlights. They were all going bunk hopping. If she didn't go, Katie would be the only one left.

All alone in the cabin at night? That was just too scary!

Katie leaped out of bed and grabbed her flashlight. "Wait up!" she whispered hoarsely.

"Now be really quiet," Alicia told them as she slowly opened the door and tiptoed down the cabin steps.

The girls all followed Alicia as she slipped behind the bunk, taking care to stay out of sight of the on-duty counselors, who were sitting at a picnic table near a tree.

"Where are we going?" Chelsea asked.

Alicia put her fingers to her lips and glared at her.

No one said a word after that.

Katie looked up at the night sky. She'd

never seen so many stars before. And they were all so bright and shiny. Katie had to admit it was kind of cool being out so late at night. The danger of sneaking around was a little thrilling. Katie had never done anything like this before!

The camp was quiet, except for the sounds of the crickets chirping and the occasional whisper or giggle from one of the on-duty counselors.

*Crack.* Just then, a twig snapped beneath Katie's feet.

"Shhh . . ." Alicia hissed.

"I . . ." Katie was about to say she was sorry, but she stopped herself. It was better to keep quiet.

The girls continued to follow Alicia. They snuck between the Stingray and Sea Horse bunks, across the athletic field, and behind the mess hall. Alicia finally stopped when they reached the nature shack. She looked around to make sure no one was around. Then she opened the door of the shack and walked inside.

"What are we doing here?" Rainbow whispered.

"I thought we'd play a little joke on Shannon," Alicia told her.

"Why would we do that?" Gianna wondered.

"Because she was so mean," Alicia said. "I had to miss the campfire, remember?"

"But she wasn't mean to the rest of us," Chelsea pointed out.

"Oh, come on, you guys, it's just a joke," Alicia told them. "I'm just gonna put a lizard in her bed. I want to see how scared she gets."

"That's not a nice thing to do—to Shannon or the lizard," Katie said.

"Don't be such babies," Alicia snarled.

"Stop calling us that!" Katie shouted back.

Alicia shrugged and walked over to the lizard cage. Slowly she removed the lid. Then she reached her hand into the cage and . . .

*Flick!* Just then the lights went on in the nature shack.

Katie gulped. This was sooo not good.

# Chapter 14

"I am really upset!" Shannon shouted after the girls returned to the bunk. The nature counselor was very angry, too. "I can't believe my girls went bunk hopping!"

Katie bit her lip. She didn't know what to say. The last thing she ever wanted to do was disappoint her counselor.

"We're sorry," Gianna said quietly.

"We just wanted to see what it felt like," Rainbow added.

"All the bigger girls do it, so . . ." Chelsea added.

"Who told you that?" Shannon asked.

No one said a word.

Shannon nodded quietly. "Well, since you girls like wandering around camp when no one else is around, I guess I should let you do that."

Katie looked at her counselor with surprise. Was she really going to say it was okay for them to go bunk hopping?

No such luck.

"Tomorrow morning you're all going to get up extra early," Shannon told them. "And then you're going to walk around the whole camp, singing. It will be your job to wake everyone else in the camp in time for breakfast."

"We have to get up early?" Chelsea exclaimed.

Shannon nodded. "And be ready to sing."

"In front of everyone?" Katie asked nervously. Somehow she didn't think she could do that.

"Oh yeah," Shannon told her. "And loudly, too. Remember, you have to get everyone up. So I guess that means you girls will want to climb into your beds and go to sleep now."

The girls all did as they were told.

After Shannon shut off the light, Alicia began to grumble. "I told you we should have put that lizard in her bed."

Katie folded her pillow over her ears so she couldn't hear her. She wasn't going to listen to anything Alicia said. Not for the rest of the summer!

"It's time to get up. It's time to get up. It's time to get up in the morning!" the Bumblebees sang out as they trudged through camp from cabin to cabin.

"Ahhh, be quiet!" someone yelled from the Sharks' bunk.

But the Bumblebees couldn't be quiet. They had to sing. And loud.

"It's time to get up. It's time to get up . . ."

"I hate Bumblebees!" someone in the

Stingray bunk screamed through the cabin window.

Katie frowned. She didn't like it when people were mad at her. And from the sound of things, the whole camp was pretty angry with the Bumblebees today. Nobody at camp liked getting out of bed in the morning. Getting woken up by a bunch of girls singing—*off-key*—was making it that much worse.

But by the time everyone got to breakfast, it seemed all had been forgiven. In fact, some of the older girls were laughing about what had happened.

"Don't feel so bad," Lexi told her. "We've all had to do that."

"Yeah," another girl from Lexi's cabin said. "And I didn't go bunk hopping until I was a Sea Horse. I think you guys are the first Bumblebees to ever have the guts to sneak out at night."

"Pretty impressive," Lexi agreed.

"Gee, thanks . . ." Katie said proudly.

"But you'd better not do it again," Lexi warned. "The next punishment will probably be even worse."

Katie was surprised. "Worse than having to sing in front of the whole camp?" she asked.

"Oh yeah. You don't want to be left out of Color War," Lexi's friend told her. "And that's what they would probably do."

That settled it. From now on, Katie was staying put after lights-out. Her bunk-hopping days were over.

# Chapter 15

Alicia, on the other hand, didn't seem to care what she was going to miss. That night Katie and the rest of the girls lay in their beds, trying to be good. But Alicia hopped out of hers and grabbed her flashlight.

"You're not going bunk hopping again, are you?" Katie asked her nervously. "You might miss Color War."

"Big deal," Alicia answered. "So I might miss a bunch of stupid relay races and singing."

"Don't listen to her," Gianna told Katie. "Color War is totally awesome. It's the most exciting part of camp!"

"Anyhow, I'm not leaving the cabin," Alicia
said. "I'm just going to remake Shannon's bed
for her."

"Why?" Rainbow asked. "It looks pretty
neat. Besides, she's just going to get into bed
in an hour or two and unmake it."

"Exactly," Alicia said with a big smile.

"Only she's going to have a tough time doing that, because I'm short-sheeting it."

"Alicia, that's not nice," Gianna warned.

"What's short-sheeting?" Chelsea asked.

"Alicia's going to fold over the top sheet so it looks normal," Gianna explained.

"Yeah," Alicia agreed. "But when she tries to climb in, she won't be able to. Pretty funny, huh?"

"Come on, Alicia, go back to bed," Gianna said.

"No way," Alicia replied.

There was no stopping Alicia when she had her mind made up. Katie picked up her flashlight and one of the comic books her grandmother had sent her in a package. She read for a while and then fell asleep.

Katie didn't know how long she'd been sleeping when she heard a rustling coming from the far end of the bunk.

She sat up suddenly. Had Rocky come back to visit?

No. That wasn't it. As she squinted in the darkness, she could hear Shannon struggling.

"Darn it," the counselor muttered as she stood up and pulled the blankets and sheets from her mattress and started to remake her bed. "AAAH!" she shouted out suddenly.

Her scream woke up the whole cabin.

"What's wrong?" Rainbow cried out.

Shannon ripped her sheets from her bed. "Someone put worms in my bed!"

"Ooh, worms. Gross," Chelsea gulped.

"I've got to shake these sheets out," Shannon said as she opened the cabin door.

A few giggles came from Alicia's bed. Alicia had her pillow over her mouth to muffle the sound, but Katie could still hear her.

"How come you're never nice, Alicia?" Katie whispered loudly.

Alicia just laughed.

But she wasn't laughing the next morning. As soon as the Bumblebees had woken up and gotten dressed, Shannon said, "You know what, girls? I found out last night that Alicia has a special talent. She is a wonderful bed maker. And to prove it, she's going to make every one of your beds today."

Alicia gasped. "I'm what?"

"You're going to make all the beds in the bunk," Shannon told her. "But not the way you made mine last night. You're going to make the beds the right way."

"I don't know what you're talking about," Alicia lied.

"Alicia, I know you short-sheeted my bed," Shannon said. "And you put the worms in there, too."

Katie bit her lip. She thought she had been whispering pretty quietly. She hadn't meant for Shannon to hear her say anything.

"Tattletale," Alicia hissed as she walked over to Katie's bed and began to straighten the covers.

# Chapter 16

"Water! I need water!" Katie exclaimed as she walked into the mess hall at lunchtime. She was hot, sweaty, and incredibly happy.

"I did it!" she told the other Bumblebees excitedly. "I served the ball over the net!"

"It was awesome!" Gianna congratulated her. "I couldn't return the ball."

"You should be proud of yourself, Katie," Shannon told her.

"I am," Katie replied. "I've been working all week to learn how to do that."

She stopped for a minute. All week. It was hard to believe that tomorrow she would be at Cedar Hill Camp for a whole week!

Which meant camp was already almost half over. That made Katie kind of sad.

But before she could think too much about that, she heard a loud banging and clanging from the mess-hall door. Then she heard wild screaming and yelling.

"COLOR WAR! COLOR WAR! COLOR WAR!"

Diana, the arts-and-crafts counselor, Maria and Jessie, two of the athletics counselors, and Carrie, the nature counselor, all came racing into the mess hall. They were banging on pots and pans and screaming at the top of their lungs.

Before long, everyone else in the mess hall was banging on the tables, too. "COLOR WAR!" they shouted. "COLOR WAR!"

Carrie jumped up on a bench and threw blue confetti in the air. Maria threw orange confetti. Diana threw green confetti. And coach Jessie added a big handful of white.

Katie looked up as the rainbow of shredded

paper fell all around her. It was so pretty and exciting. "COLOR WAR!" she shouted louder.

The nature counselor picked up a microphone. "Well, I guess you know that Color War has broken," she said.

Everyone started to cheer.

"To find out what color your team is, look inside the can in the middle of your table," the nature counselor continued.

Until that moment Katie hadn't even noticed the tin can on the table. She'd been too excited about what had happened at tennis. But now even that didn't seem all that important. Nothing did—except finding out what color team the Bumblebees were on.

Chelsea leaped up and grabbed the can. She twisted the top open and . . .

*BOING!* A big green rubber snake jumped out of the can.

"Aaah!" Chelsea shrieked.

"I guess we're on the Green team," Rainbow said, laughing.

"Gee, you're a real genius," Alicia said. She was trying to sound bored. But Katie could tell she was excited about Color War, too.

"Team meetings begin after lunch," Carrie announced to everyone. "The races start tonight. Get ready for two and a half days of crazy competitions. It's going to be a fight to the finish!"

"I got it!" Shannon announced a few hours later as she raced into the bunk with a brown paper bag in her hands. She reached into the bag and took out a can of bright green hair dye. She had driven to a nearby town with a couple of other counselors for some Color War supplies.

"You're absolutely sure this will come out, right?" Chelsea asked nervously.

"Absolutely," Shannon assured her. "It says right here that it washes out with just one shampoo."

Katie reached into her cubby and pulled out a disposable camera. "I'm so glad my grandma sent me this in a package. I want to remember this always."

"We'd better do this outside," Shannon told the girls, picking up the bag of green hair color and heading out of the bunk.

"Hey, where's Alicia?" Gianna asked as the girls followed their counselor out of the bunk.

"She went for a walk," Chelsea said. "The only race she's in is the swim marathon, and that's tomorrow. She doesn't feel like she has to be around for the rest of the stuff."

"She's on the Green team," Rainbow said. "She should be here to cheer for her teammates."

"Alicia's on the Alicia team," Gianna groaned. "She doesn't care about anyone else."

"Well, I'm not going to let her spoil my fun," Chelsea said, spraying some bright green color on her braids. "I'm in tonight's softball game. And I'm planning on hitting a home run."

"I'm in the water-balloon toss," Rainbow said.

"I'll come cheer you on," Gianna said. "My races don't start until tomorrow. I'm in the rowboat race and the canoe race."

"How about you, Katie?" Rainbow asked.

"I'm in the obstacle course tomorrow," Katie told her. "And I'm on the arts-and-crafts committee—I'm going to help make our banner for the big sing."

"I can't wait for the sing," Shannon said.

"It's the best part."

Katie couldn't wait, either. At the team meeting the counselors had explained what a sing was.

On the last night of Color War, all the teams got together on the tennis courts. Each team had a chance to sing one song and give one cheer. The cheer had to be one the girls made up. They also had to show their team banners. A group of judges voted on whose was the best.

At the end of the evening, after the judges added up the points from all the races and the sing, they announced the winner of Color War. And finally, there would be fireworks over the lake!

"GREEN TEAM! GREEN TEAM!" Shannon began to cheer as she sprayed some green dye on her bangs.

"WOO! WOO!" Katie screamed as she covered her red hair with green dye. "GREEN TEAM! GREEN TEAM!"

# Chapter 17

"Go, Chelsea, go!" Katie shouted as she watched her friend run toward second base during the evening softball game. "Faster! Faster!"

"I can't believe she hit a double!" Rainbow exclaimed excitedly.

"She's really good," Katie observed.

Alicia shrugged and scratched at her arm. "She's all right."

"Oh, and you could do better?" Gianna asked her.

"I'll do fine in the swim marathon," Alicia told her. "I always do." She scratched lazily at a mosquito bite on her knee.

"Boy, you must have been out in the sun too long today," Katie told Alicia. "Your face is kind of red."

"Yeah, well, yours is kind of green," Alicia snapped back.

"That's paint from the arts-and-crafts shack. I've been working on the team banner," Katie explained. "It's really pretty."

"Sure," Alicia said sarcastically.

"I'll bet it's a great banner," Rainbow told Katie. "I can't wait to see it."

"I have to go finish it tomorrow," Katie told Rainbow. "So I might not be able to come cheer for you at the water-balloon toss."

"That's okay," Rainbow assured her. "You'll be there in spirit."

"Man, these mosquitoes are really biting tonight," Alicia said.

"I haven't gotten bitten yet," Rainbow said.

"Me neither," Katie agreed.

"Maybe these mosquitoes just don't like baby blood," Alicia said. "Because they're biting me."

Katie frowned. She was tired of Alicia being so mean all the time. She was sick of being called a baby. "You should be glad you're getting bitten," Katie told her. "At least the mosquitoes like you. No one else does."

"Whoa! Good one, Katie!" Gianna congratulated her.

"That was funny," Rainbow added.

But Alicia didn't seem to think it was funny. In fact, Katie was pretty sure she saw her face get even redder.

Suddenly Katie felt bad. She didn't like hurting anyone's feelings. Not even Alicia's. What was the matter? It was as if Alicia tried to make people not like her.

"Rise and shine!" Shannon exclaimed happily early the next morning. "It's a beautiful day for a Color War!"

One by one the Bumblebees crawled out of their beds. Katie went to her cubby and sleepily pulled out her green-and-white polka-dot shirt and green shorts. She pulled her hair into a ponytail and wrapped Chelsea's green hair bow around it.

By breakfast time the other Bumblebees were also dressed in green from head to toe.

All except Alicia. She was still lying in bed.

"My head hurts," she told Shannon. "Can't I just sleep through breakfast?"

"You might feel better if you eat something," Shannon suggested. "You'll need all the energy you can get for your swimming race."

Alicia just groaned. "Man, these mosquito bites really itch!" she said as she popped out of bed.

"You can go to sick call at the infirmary after breakfast and get some lotion to put on them," Shannon suggested.

"That stuff never works," Alicia complained.

"Well, it's the best we have," Shannon said, trying to sound cheerful. "Besides, that cool lake water will make you feel better."

"I won't be in there very long," Alicia told her. "I'll win that race so fast, I'll be out before anyone knows what's happening."

Katie thought that sounded pretty stuck-up. But Shannon didn't seem to.

"That's the spirit!" the counselor said cheerfully. "Go, Green!"

Breakfast during Color War sure was loud. All the girls cheered for their teams, practically forgetting about their eggs and juice. (Of course, camp eggs were pretty forgettable anyway!)

"Hurry up, we've got to get to our races!" Gianna told the other Bumblebees.

"Chill out," Alicia argued. "We don't get points for finishing first in breakfast."

"I can't eat," Rainbow said. "I'm too stressed out about the water-balloon toss."

"You'll be great," Shannon assured her. "Mighty Green will reign supreme!"

"Oh no, is it raining?" Rainbow asked.

"Not that kind of rain, ding-dong," Alicia said. "Reign. It means rule."

"Don't call her a ding-dong," Chelsea shouted at Alicia.

"I'll call her anything I want," Alicia argued.

Katie sighed. She was sooo tired of all the fighting that Alicia caused. "Shannon, I have to go to arts and crafts and get working on the banner," Katie told her counselor. "Can I be excused?"

Shannon nodded. "Sure can. Go, Green!"

# Chapter 18

The camp was quiet as Katie walked into the arts-and-crafts shack. Everyone was still in the mess hall finishing breakfast.

But Katie didn't mind the silence. In fact, it was kind of a relief to be by herself.

Katie pulled out the green paint and found the banner she had been working on. Suddenly she felt a cool breeze blowing on the back of her neck. At first she was happy about that. It was nice to feel some fresh air on such a hot, sticky day.

But then Katie noticed that the wind didn't seem to be blowing anywhere else. Not in the trees. Not in the grass. Just on her.

The magic wind was back! Katie wasn't going to be herself for much longer.

"Oh no! Not now. Not during Color War!" Katie shouted out. But the magic wind didn't stop blowing. In fact, it blew faster and faster, spinning wildly just around Katie.

And then it stopped. Just like that.

Katie Carew was gone. One, two, switcheroo.

She was someone else.

But who?

Katie didn't even have to open her eyes to figure that out. Her itchy mosquito-bitten arms and legs told her right away!

Katie had turned into Alicia—right before the big race.

This was sooo not good. There was no way Katie could win the swim marathon. She'd never been to the raft in the middle of the lake before.

And now was not the time to try it.

Katie was not going to try to be Alicia in

the race. She knew what a disaster *that* could wind up being.

Like the time she switcherooed into Kevin before his big karate tournament. She hadn't been able to break a board. In fact she hadn't even hit the board. Instead she'd missed and landed on her tush.

And then there was the time the magic wind turned her into Suzanne during a fashion show. She'd put her pants on backward and walked down the runway like Frankenstein in those awful high heels. Suzanne was so embarrassed—and it hadn't even been her fault.

But a swim race? This could be the biggest disaster of all time.

Katie didn't like Alicia. But she didn't want to make a fool out of her. She had to find a place to hide. A safe place where no one could find her.

How about the woods?

No. That wouldn't work. It was scary out

there. And besides, that was against the rules.

The bunk! That was it. No one would be there. Everyone was out at Color War activities.

Quickly Katie raced to the Bumblebee bunk, taking care not to be seen by anyone.

*Phew.* A few minutes later she was safe inside. No one could find her.

Or could they?

# Chapter 19

*Clomp. Clomp. Clomp.*

Suddenly Katie heard footsteps coming up
the stairs toward the bunk. Oh no! Someone
was coming. Quickly she dove beneath the
bottom bunk of Alicia's bed.

If she stayed really still, maybe she
wouldn't be noticed. Because if she was seen,
she would be taken for Alicia and would be
forced to swim.

But staying still wasn't easy. Katie's nose
was right up against one of Alicia's smelly
gym socks. She'd thrown it under there
instead of sending it to the laundry. A skunk
would have smelled better than that sock did.

But Katie couldn't move the sock. Any move could reveal her hiding place.

"I haven't seen Alicia anywhere," Katie heard Chelsea say.

"Me neither. I checked the mess hall, the nature shack, and the canteen," she heard Rainbow add.

"Leave it to Alicia to mess up Color War for us," Gianna added.

"Maybe Katie's seen her," Chelsea suggested.

Katie frowned. Seen her? She *was* her.

And at the moment, being Alicia was getting more and more difficult. Alicia never swept under her bed. The dust bunnies made Katie want to sneeze.

The mosquito bites all over Alicia's body were making Katie itch.

And that smelly sock was making her kinda sick to her stomach.

But Katie didn't dare sneeze, scratch, or puke.

"Katie's in arts and crafts working on the banner," Rainbow told Chelsea. "Alicia wouldn't go there." She plopped down on the bed just above Katie. The mattress sank down right in the middle, hitting Katie on the back.

"Mmmph . . ." Katie let out a small groan, shoving her fist in her mouth to muffle the sound.

"Did you hear that?" Chelsea asked nervously.

Katie's heart began to pound. What if the

girls found her now? They'd make her swim for sure. What a mess that would be!

"Come on, Chels, there are no ghosts here," Rainbow said in her gentle voice. She shifted her weight slightly. Now the mattress sank into the back of Katie's head. That pushed her face farther into the stinky sock. *Blech!*

"This is the worst thing Alicia has ever done," Gianna said. "The Green team is in second place. We need Alicia to win that race to pull us into first."

"I know. All the older girls on our team are in the soccer match," Rainbow said. "We have no one to swim in that race."

The girls all looked at one another and frowned.

"Oh yes, we do!" Chelsea exclaimed suddenly. She jumped up.

"Where are you going?" Shannon asked her.

"To put on my bathing suit," Chelsea replied. "I'm taking Alicia's place."

"But you can't swim," Gianna reminded her.

Chelsea shook her head. "I never said I *couldn't* swim. I said I didn't *want* to swim. I've been swimming since I was four years old. I'm really good—and fast."

"But what about your hair?" Rainbow asked her.

Chelsea shrugged. "This is an emergency. But my blow-dryer better be working when I get back!"

# Chapter 20

*"AAACHOOO!"*

The second the girls left the bunk, Katie let out the biggest sneeze of her whole life. Then she scratched the mosquito bites on her legs and took a deep breath of fresh air.

It was good to be out from under the bed.

Hopefully no one would come back to the bunk. But just in case, Katie decided to stay on the floor near Alicia's bed.

And that's when she noticed the diary on the floor next to Alicia's bed. It must have fallen out from her cubby. Now there it was, lying open on the floor.

Katie knew it was wrong to read someone

else's diary. *Really* wrong. But it was lying there, wide open.

She couldn't help taking a peek.

Alicia had written a poem on one of the pretty pink pages.

*No letters for me again today.*
*It's no surprise I have to say.*
*I never hear from Mom and Dad.*
*Do they know it makes me sad?*
*Not even one letter.*
*Mosquitoes like me better.*

Katie thought back to all the times Shannon had brought the mail to the bunk. She hadn't really noticed it before, but Alicia never seemed to get any letters or packages like everyone else did.

No wonder she was so angry all the time.

Just then Katie heard lots and lots of cheering. It was coming from the waterfront area. The big swim marathon was on!

Katie really wanted to be down there at the lake cheering on her bunkmate. But she couldn't. Not as long as she was Alicia.

Still, she sure wanted to know who was winning.

A few minutes later Katie had her answer. One of the swim counselors shouted the results through a megaphone:

"First place: Blue team.

Second place: Green team.

Third place: Orange team.

Fourth place: White team."

Wow. Second place was great. Especially since Chelsea hadn't been swimming all summer.

But it wasn't enough to bring the Green team to first place.

Just then, Katie felt a breeze blowing on the back of her neck. The cool wind felt nice as it gently blew on her.

But then, suddenly, the breeze wasn't so gentle anymore. It was getting stronger and stronger. Now it was a powerful tornado. *A tornado that was swirling just around Katie.*

The magic wind was back! It whirled and swirled, lifting Katie's legs right off the ground.

And then it stopped. Just like that. Katie was back.

So was Alicia. And, boy, was she surprised.

"What am I doing here?" Alicia asked Katie.

"You . . . uh . . . you came back to the bunk to . . ." Katie didn't know what to tell her. There was no way she could explain this.

Luckily, Alicia wasn't waiting for an explanation. She looked at the alarm clock on top of Shannon's cubby and gulped. "Oh man, I'm late. I was supposed to be at the lake twenty minutes ago. I've got to get my bathing suit on and get down there."

"Don't bother," Rainbow said as she and the other Bumblebees walked into the bunk. "The race is over."

"Chelsea swam in your place," Gianna added.

Alicia bit her lip. "How did you do?" she asked Chelsea.

"Second place," Chelsea replied proudly. "Not bad, considering it's the first time I swam all summer."

"I would have come in first," Alicia murmured quietly.

"Yeah, well, you weren't there. You let us

down," Gianna yelled at her.

Katie looked over at Alicia. She looked as if she was going to cry. And the saddest part was that it wasn't even Alicia's fault. It was Katie's fault. *She* was the one who had chickened out of swimming.

Now, because of Katie, the rest of the bunk hated Alicia even more than before.

"We're going to have to win the big sing tomorrow," Rainbow said.

"Our team song is really good," Chelsea said.

"But we don't have a cheer yet," Gianna reminded her. "It's got to be the best ever if we want to win the sing."

That gave Katie an idea. "Our cheer will be awesome," Katie said. "Because Alicia's going to write it. She's a great writer."

Alicia looked at her curiously. "I am?"

"You write poems in your diary, don't you?" Katie said.

"How did you know that?" Alicia asked

angrily. "Were you snooping in my cubby?"

*Oops.* "I . . . um . . . I just figured that was what you were writing in there. Because, uh . . . well . . . you're too smart and cool to just write sentences like other people," Katie said quickly.

Alicia stared at her in surprise. The other girls looked pretty shocked, too. No one ever complimented Alicia.

"Why should we let *her* write our cheer?" Gianna asked Katie. "She's the reason we're in this mess, anyway. She's the one who ran out on us before the race. But you did a great job, too, Chelsea," she added, making sure her friend's feelings weren't hurt.

"Thanks," Chelsea replied. "But even I know Alicia could have won it. She just didn't want to."

"No, that's not it," Alicia insisted. "I didn't feel . . . well . . . actually, I'm not sure what happened."

"Come on, haven't any of you guys ever

gotten really nervous about something?" Katie added, covering for Alicia. "She just freaked out."

"I did?" Alicia looked totally puzzled.

"Anyway, Alicia can make it up to us by writing the cheer," Katie said.

"I guess we could give her a chance," Rainbow said.

"But don't mess it up," Chelsea added.

"I won't," Alicia vowed. "I promise."

# Chapter 21

"Blue rules! The rest are fools! Gooo, Blue!"

While the Blue team finished their cheer at the sing, the Green team took the stage.

Katie, Alicia, Rainbow, Gianna, and Chelsea all had green paint in their hair. They'd used face paint to draw green stripes on their faces. Some of the older girls were practically painted from head to toe in green.

"They look like big pickles," Alicia said.

The Bumblebees all giggled. They knew it was a joke. Alicia wasn't being mean at all.

"Thanks for coming up with a way for me to be part of Color War," Alicia whispered to

Katie. For the first time she sounded really nice.

"The Green team needs you," Katie replied. "You're going to lead us to victory!"

Suddenly Shannon came running over to them. "Okay, girls, it's time for the Green team to do their cheer."

Katie looked over at Alicia. "Ready?"

Alicia nodded. "You bet!"

"Then let's go!"

With Alicia leading the way, the members of the Green team began their cheer.

"Mighty Greens,

We're the Color War queens.

Toughest girls you've ever seen,

Other teams shake,

Their boots quake,

When we take the lead

With killer speed.

It's like nothing you've ever seen,

The mean Green fighting machine!"

A few minutes later, after all the teams had sung their songs and shouted their cheers, the judges announced the winner.

"And in first place, the Green team!"

All at once everyone on the Green team began screaming, shouting, and hugging one another.

Some of the bigger girls picked up Alicia and began carrying her around on their shoulders.

Alicia was a hero. She had led the Green team to victory.

Well, actually, she and Katie had done that—since it had been Katie's idea. But Katie was fine with letting Alicia take the credit. It was the first time she had seen her friend smile all summer.

*Friend.* Wow. That was a word Katie never thought she would use to describe Alicia. But Alicia *was* her friend now.

And, as if to prove it, Alicia whispered something in one of the older girls' ears. A

moment later three big girls raced over and lifted Katie off the ground, too.

"Yeah, Alicia! Yeah, Katie!" they shouted loudly.

"Yeah, Green team!" Katie and Alicia cheered back.

# Chapter 22

As Katie stepped onto the yellow school bus, she turned and took one last look around. She couldn't believe camp was over. But Katie wasn't sad. She knew she would be back next summer. And so would Alicia, Rainbow, Gianna, and Chelsea. They had all promised to return to Camp Cedar Hill.

Suddenly a song began running through Katie's head. "Friends, friends, friends. We will always be . . ." she hummed to herself as she found a seat in the middle of the bus.

A few minutes later, the bus driver turned on the engine and started driving home toward Cherrydale.

Katie reached into her backpack and pulled out a white pillowcase. The other Bumblebees had all signed and written their addresses and phone numbers on it. Katie found the address she was looking for and pulled out one last postcard.

She was making sure her friend Alicia got at least *one* letter this summer.

Dear Alicia,

I hope the rest of your summer is a lot of fun. I am going to spend this whole month practicing my swimming at our town pool. Next year I will take the deepwater swim test so we can swim together. I hope you can visit me in Cherrydale this winter.

Your pal,

Katie

P.S. Go, Green team!

# You G·O·TT·A Have It!

Overnight camps usually send out a list of items they think you need to pack in your trunk. You've probably seen the kinds of things they put on their lists: 14 pairs of underwear, 10 pairs of shorts, 10 camp T-shirts, 18 pairs of socks . . .

Sure, you need that stuff, but doesn't it sound so *boring*?

Of course, there are plenty of items camps forget to tell you to stash in your luggage. Those are the kinds of things any camper will need to *really* survive the summer. That's why Katie and her friends have designed this Gotta Have It Checklist. Pack the items on the list, and your summer can't miss!

Aren't you lucky to have pals like the Bumblebees of Camp Cedar Hill?

## ☑ THE GOTTA HAVE IT CHECKLIST

✗ Scented stickers (to seal the envelopes for your letters to the friends and folks back home)

✗ A photo of your pet (Katie kissed Pepper's picture every day she was away!)

✗ A favorite sleep friend (don't be embarrassed to bring your teddy bear along—everyone does!)

✗ A disposable camera (to keep your memories alive even after you get home)

✗ Extra hair ribbons, clips, and bows (you'd be surprised how quickly they disappear!)

- ✕ Posters and paper flowers (to decorate the bunk)
- ✕ Tape (to put up the posters and paper flowers, of course)
- ✕ Face paints (so you can paint your face for Color War)
- ✕ A book of creepy ghost stories (to read late at night)
- ✕ A book of jokes (just in case your bunkmates are too creeped out by your ghost stories)
- ✕ An extra plain white pillowcase for your pals to sign (it's the perfect end-of-summer souvenir!)

# About the Author

**NANCY KRULIK** is the author of more than 150 books for children and young adults, including three *New York Times* bestsellers. She lives in New York City with her husband, composer Daniel Burwasser, their children, Amanda and Ian, and Pepper, a chocolate and white spaniel mix. When she's not busy writing the *Katie Kazoo, Switcheroo* series, Nancy loves swimming, reading, and going to the movies.

# About the Illustrators

**JOHN & WENDY'S** art has been featured in other books for children, in magazines, on stationery, and on toys. When they are not drawing Katie and her friends, they like to paint, take photographs, travel, and play music in their rock-'n'-roll band. They live and work in Brooklyn, New York.